D0597437

D

# THE Circus

## HEIDI GOENNEL

Tambourine Books · New York

The full-color illustrations were painted in acrylic on canvas.

Library of Congress Cataloging in Publication Data
Goennel, Heidi.   The circus/by Heidi Goennel.
p.   cm.
Summary: A child describes the wonderful sights at a circus.
ISBN 0-688-10883-0 (trade)—ISBN 0-688-10884-9 (lib.)
[1. Circus—Fiction.] I. Title.
PZ7.G554Ci  1992  [E]—dc20  91-448  CIP  AC

1  3  5  7  9  10  8  6  4  2
First edition

26,892

For F.L.

The circus comes to town every year.

Early in the morning we watch the tent go up.

We see acrobats and jugglers practice near the wild animals.

The tiger growls "Hello" as we buy our tickets.

Before the show we get some peanuts.
Then we hurry to our seats.

"Welcome to the circus!" says the Ringmaster.

Pretty ladies on white horses gallop into the ring.

And next, the Lion Tamer shows us how brave he is.

The acrobats on the flying trapeze soar way above our heads.

Look, on the tightrope a man rides a unicycle while he juggles six balls.

The elephants come next. See, a baby one is at the end.

At last it's time for the clowns and their silly dogs.

And then the big parade ends the show.

We can't wait until the circus comes back next year.